The Thrill Points Race

written by Jamie Michalak

Based on the motion picture screenplay
by Megan McDonald and Kathy Waugh

Based on the Judy Moody series by Megan McDonald

CANDLEWICK PRESS

Based on the theatrical motion picture *Judy Moody and the NOT Bummer Summer,*
produced by Smokewood Entertainment

First edition 2011

ISBN 978-0-7636-5552-5

11 12 13 14 15 16 WOR 10 9 8 7 6 5 4 3 2 1

Printed in Stevens Point, WI, U.S.A.

This book was typeset in ITC Cheltamham and Judy Moody.

Candlewick Press
99 Dover Street
Somerville, Massachusetts 02144

visit us at www.candlewick.com
www.judymoodythemovie.com

Contents

Hi from
HUNTER RULEZ

CHAPTER ONE

A RARE Idea

Judy Moody was in a mood. A yay for the last day of school mood! Her teacher, Mr. Todd, told the class that he had a brand-new summer job.

"If you find out what it is before the end of the summer, you'll win a prize," he said.

"We need a clue!" Judy said.

"Clue, clue, clue, clue!" repeated the class.

"Okay, okay," said Mr. Todd. "The clue is . . . COLD. Brrr!"

Then *brrr-iiiinnnng!* School was O-V-E-R!

After school, Judy met her friends Rocky, Amy, and Frank met in the tent in her backyard.

"I have a DARE-ing idea," she told them. "We are going to have the most way-rare double-cool NOT bummer summer ever!"

"What's the plan?" Frank asked.

Moody
MEGA-RARE NOT
Bummer Summer Dare!
Thrill Points
Bonus Points!
Loser Points
Big Fat Total!!
DARES
RIDE
Scream
Monster
Surf
a
Wave

"Dares are something way fun that we've never done before," she said. She held up a chart. "For every dare we do, we get ten thrill points—plus bonus points for extra-daring dares. And we lose points if something goes wrong. When we reach one hundred points, then—presto whammo—we've had the best summer ever!"

"But Rocky's going away to circus camp for the summer," Amy said.

"Amy's going away, too," Rocky said. "To Borneo!"

Judy couldn't believe her ears.

"What's Borneo?" Judy asked. "You guys are making that up."

"Nuh-uh. It's an island—all the way across the world," said Amy.

“Great,” said Judy. “Just great.” Now she’d be stuck with Frank “Eats-Paste” Pearl and her little “bother,” Stink, all bummer summer long.

The next day Judy’s parents told her that they were going to California to help her grandparents move.

“You’re going to leave me here alone—with Stink?” Judy asked.

"Of course not, Judy," said Mom. "Aunt Opal's coming to stay with you."

"Aunt Awful? I don't even know her!" said Judy. *She could be a zombie!* she thought.

But when Aunt Opal arrived later that week, she was super-cool. She even brought presents. As in NOT birthday

gifts. As in cool stuff. Stink got a book about how to find and catch Bigfoot, and Judy got a mega-glam mood ring. She put it on. The stone was red for *Love.* Rare!

Aunt Opal also gave Judy an awesome idea for how to have a NOT-bummer summer even though her friends were away. They didn't have to do dares together. They could earn thrill points on their own!

Judy e-mailed Amy and Rocky:

Let's do the dare race, starting right NOW! First one to get 100 points WINS!

Rocky wrote back right away:

I'm in. Check out what I did today!

He sent a picture of himself walking on a tightrope. That was ten points for sure.

The thrill race was ON.

ROANOKE
CIRCUS CAMP

CHAPTER TWO

The Great Judy-a-Rini

Judy told Frank the new plan.

"What's the first dare?" he asked.

"This," said Judy. She showed him the picture of Rocky on the tightrope.

"We're going to circus camp, too?"

"NO," said Judy. "We are going to walk on a tightrope like Rocky did."

Judy tied one end of a rope to a tree in her backyard. They stretched it across the creek and tied it to a tree on the other side. Ta-da! Instant tightrope!

Judy climbed onto the rope.

"Now, the high-flying, death-defying Judy-a-Rini will cross Niagara Falls!" she said. "One slip, and she'll fall to her doom!"

The rope wiggled.

Judy wobbled.

"Don't worry!" said Judy. "The great Judy-a-Rini WILL NOT FALL— "

Judy looked back. Frank was on the rope now, too!

She took another step.

"MOSQUITOS!" cried Frank.

"Stop WOBBLING me!" said Judy.

"I can't help it! There's a mosquito on my—"

SPLASH! went Frank.

SPLOOSH! went Judy.

Total thrill points = zero.

The next day, Judy had another idea: Ride the Scream Monster at the amusement park! A roller coaster equals thrill points for sure.

"Bonus points for no hands," she told Frank when they got to the park.

But Frank had already bought a corn dog, cotton candy, two ice-cream cones, and a snow cone.

When it was their turn to ride the Scream Monster, Judy and Frank stepped forward.

"No food on the ride," the ticket guy said to Frank.

"What? No way am I throwing this stuff out!"

"Frank!" said Judy. "We've got to start earning thrill points!"

Frank gulped down one bite of everything, then threw the rest away.

He hopped into the seat next to Judy.

"This is it!" said Judy. "Thrill points here we come!"

Their car inched up the hill.

Click-click-click-click-click.

"Hands up!" said Judy. "Every second counts!"

"I'm not so sure about this," said Frank.

"Too late now," said Judy. "Because here we goooooooooooooooo!"

WHOOSH! went the Scream Monster.

"Ahhhh!" went Judy.

"AHHHHHH!" went Frank.

Judy looked over at Frank. Frank looked sick.

"No!" she said. "Don't you . . . DARE!" But Frank did. *BLUCK!* A stream of blue spurted out of his mouth . . . and all over Judy.

"Ew, ew, EW!" Judy cried. "Puke Monster!"

It was a P.U. ride home.

10 Scream Monster points – 10 points for blue throw up = No thrill points!

CHAPTER THREE

Fun Sponge

Over the next few weeks, Judy Moody tried tons of dares. But no matter what, something always went wrong, and she still had a big fat ZERO for points. She even made crazy hats out of garbage-can lids with Aunt Opal. They were going to sneak them onto the stone lions in front of the library! But then Judy's hand got glued to the table instead.

So she still had no points. Nada, zip, zilch. And one super-sticky hand.

Meanwhile, Rocky and Amy had MEGA points. Amy swam with a shark—scary points! Rocky learned how to saw someone in half—magic points!

Judy had one more THRILL-ing idea. They were showing an Evil Creature Double Feature at the movie theater the next night. Two scary movies and you had to wear a monster costume!

"No being a wimpburger," Judy told Frank as they got their tickets. "We have to stay till the end to get points."

They sat down and the lights went out.

Judy's mood ring was amber for *Nervous, Tense.*

The movie started. On screen, zombies slowly walked through a town, moaning and groaning. One yelled, "Hungry! I come for you!"

Frank stood up. "I have to go home. I forgot to feed my goldfish."

"Sit down!" said Judy.

But Frank ran out of the theater. Judy chased after him.

"Rocky and Amy are having the best summer ever!" she yelled at him. "And I'm stuck with Frankenscreamer!"

“Look who’s talking!” said Frank. “Your points and dares suck the fun out of everything! You’re like a big, wet . . . FUN SPONGE!”

Judy had never seen Frank mad before.

“Well, if I’m a fun sponge, then

you're a fun . . . MOP!" she said, but Frank had already started walking home.

Judy tried to go back into the theater, but her ticket was inside—and so was her backpack!

"No ticket, no movie," the ticket taker said.

Great! thought Judy. *Now I've lost my backpack, too.* So she stomped home.

She walked right past Stink and Aunt Opal, who were making a HUGE Bigfoot statue on the lawn.

"Wanna help?" asked Stink.

But Judy Moody was in a mood. "I'm spending the rest of this bummer summer in my room!" she shouted. Even her mood ring was dark blue for *Mad!*

WH20
7
WH20
7

CHAPTER FOUR

Thrill-o-Rama!

Judy was still pouting in her room the next day when she heard something outside.

"TESTING, TESTING!"

A TV reporter was talking to Stink about Bigfoot!

Judy ran downstairs.

"If you do catch Bigfoot, Mr. Stink Moody," said the reporter, "you'll be the most famous kid in America."

Catching Bigfoot would be worth a million thrill points! Judy thought.

So she went to Stink's Bigfoot club meeting that afternoon. Zeke, the leader of the club, told Stink and Judy to have a stakeout. A Bigfoot stakeout.

"Thrill-o-RAMA!" said Judy.

That night they camped out in the backyard and waited for Bigfoot. Judy had binoculars and Stink wore his berry bush disguise.

Judy heard a noise.

“Stink! Wake up!” she said.

Something was walking toward them.

“Holy macaroni! It’s him! It’s BIGFOOT!” yelled Judy.

She ran out of the tent.

“GOTCHA!”

“Aggggowwwwhhhh!” it yelled.

Stink ran over and turned on his flashlight. It wasn’t Bigfoot. It was Frank.

"I was just dropping off the back-pack you left at the movie theater," Frank said.

Suddenly, something went *CRACK!* in the woods.

"Bigfoot!" cried Judy and Stink.

"Let's go!" said Judy. "Are you coming, Frank? It's worth mega-mega points!"

But Frank had already run back to his father's car.

"Mr. Bigfoot?" Stink called. "We come in peace!"

Something hairy brushed against Judy's head.

"AHHHHHH!" she screamed.

But it wasn't Bigfoot. It was just a possum. *One possum = Zero thrill points.*

The next day, Judy had given up on finding Bigfoot when, out of nowhere, a tall, hairy creature ran past the window. A pack of dogs was chasing him down the street.

"BIGFOOT!" yelled Stink. "After him!"

Judy, Stink, and Aunt Opal joined the chase.

Then Bigfoot hopped into an ice-cream truck.

So Judy, Stink, and Aunt Opal hopped onto a bicycle.

They chased the truck all over town. At last, it stopped.

Judy couldn't believe her eyes!

"Mr. Todd!" she said. Mr. Todd was the ice-cream man! "And . . . Zeke?"

Mr. Todd explained that his summer job was to sell ice cream. He had asked Zeke to dress as Bigfoot to help attract customers.

"I found you!" Judy cried. "Do I get the prize?"

Mr. Todd gave Judy tickets to the circus. Super-cool! Judy invited Frank to come with her.

"Sorry I was such a fun sponge," she said.

"It's okay," said Frank.

Too bad she still had NADA thrill points.

But Aunt Opal had an idea! She and Judy snuck out to the library at night. They placed the garbage-can hats they had made on top of the super-serious-looking lion statues.

Homemade trash-can hats on library lions = 10 thrill points! Judy's mood ring turned purple—finally!—for *Joyful, On Top of the World.*

THRILL-A-DELIC times ten!